UNDER ALEX'S BED

UNDER ALEX'S BED
YOUNG BOY'S AMAZING JOURNEY

by
KAREN SHARP

XULON PRESS

Xulon Press
2301 Lucien Way #415
Maitland, FL 32751
407.339.4217
www.xulonpress.com

Printed in the United States of America.

ISBN-13: 978-1-6312-9287-3

TABLE OF CONTENTS

UNDER ALEX'S BED

"**W**here is that rotten knife?" Alex muttered as he pushed himself underneath his twin bed. "I've got to find it. It's gotta be here somewhere!"

Alex's mother entered the bedroom, sidestepping the clutter as if walking through a minefield. "This is truly a young boy's haven," she mused, while shaking her head in disbelief at the debris everywhere. Tons of scattered papers buried the wall-to-wall carpet, and piles of broken toys with remnants of last week's "building project" added the finishing touches of a room that had the earmark of a battleground.

Having heard bits and pieces of his monologue, she chuckled. "You couldn't find your right hand from your left in this mess," she stated. "But since you're down there, you might as well clean it up. Alex, this room should be condemned! I'm tempted to clean it up myself but afraid of the wildlife that I might encounter!" Karen smiled.

"And I figure that a ten-year-old grown man like yourself would be much more suited to battle the evil, under-the-bed monsters than an old lady like me! Hey, you might even have to protect me from them! And then, I'd be afraid that I might fall into the bad, old black hole. You know the one, don't you? That black hole under your bed? I guess I should be grateful that you haven't fallen into it yet, considering the state of your bedroom!" She laughed as she toed a pile of dirty clothes heaped on the floor.

Alex stopped squirming and popped his head out from under the bed. "What are you talking about, Mom? What black hole?" He rolled his eyes and continued. "Good grief, Mom, I really have to meet the guys back at the fort, and I really need my knife. I don't have time to clean this stupid old room right now. Can't I do it later? I promise I'll do it tonight when it's dark."

Alex paused and grinned. "And, Mom, I hope this doesn't surprise you too much, but the only black holes that are around are in *space*, not under my bed. So don't you even try that stupid kiddie stuff with me!"

Karen looked at her boy and shook her head. "No, Alex, I think you need to clean this mess up now. There is really no excuse for a room to look like this, not even a little boy's. Your friends can wait. If you hurry but do a good job, you'll be done in no time at all."

Alex groaned and pushed the rest of himself out from under the bed.

He's growing so fast, thought Karen, *and he's looking more like Mike every year*. Tousled sandy hair, unruly even when combed, was her late husband's trademark, and that, along with Alex's green eyes and slender build, testified to his father's genes. As lonely as she was for the husband she dearly missed, she was grateful that her little boy was a blessed visual reminder of him.

Karen again kicked at the clutter on the floor. "Alex, do you think I'm making it up about the black hole? Well, let me tell you that I'm not. My grandfather—your great-grandfather, Rudolph

Olson—told me about it when I was a little girl. I remember the day he walked into my bedroom, shook his head, and then asked me to sit down as he had a story to tell me. He said that he had been told this story when he was little by his daddy. Grandpa explained that the space under a bed was special and that it could be good or bad; if the room was clean, then all would be good, but if it was a mess like this room is, then it would be bad. He said that a good friend of his had had a bedroom that was a bad mess, even worse than his own, and his friend ended up missing. The police searched and even had bloodhounds out, but he was never found. Grandpa was told that his friend had fallen down a black hole that was under his bed. At first he laughed, just as you did, as he did not believe in such a silly story, but as the months passed and his friend was never found, he decided to keep his room clean!"

Alex scowled at his mother. "Gee, Mom, I know you want me to clean my room, but stupid stories about scary holes under my bed is really pushing it! I promise on Boy Scout's honor that I will clean it later if I can go now. Please? The guys are waiting on me."

"No, Alex, you can finish it now." Karen turned to leave the room. "Now hurry, and you won't miss a thing. And don't you even think about sneaking out that window! By the way, I was never told how to rescue anyone who had fallen down a black hole, so I guess you better be careful because I would be a basket case if you disappeared under that bed!" Karen covered her mouth to stifle her laugh as she hurried out of the room.

Alex was furious! He kicked at a mountain of paper and sent it flying while hurling a matchbox car across the floor. "I can't believe she tried that on me! I'm not a stupid little kid who believes fairy tales! And I can't believe that I have to stay here and clean this dumb room. Man, the guys are gonna be so mad at me, and it's all because of that dumb knife! Where is it? I'm gonna find it now, and then I'm going out that window. Mom will be mad, but she won't stay mad for long."

Pushing himself under the bed again, Alex blindly squirmed through another ocean of rubble. Old books, last year's writing assignments, paper planes that had taken a death plunge and were crinkled into wads, gum and candy wrappers, there seemed to be no end to the junk.

Then straight ahead, Alex saw it! The knife! "There you are, you pain-in-the-butt knife! I'm gonna get you now, and then I'm outta here! Mom will just have to..."

Alex never finished his sentence for as he reached for his prized Swiss Army knife, the floor seemed to give way. Confused, he whimpered, "What?" Then he screamed, "Help! Mom!"

CHAPTER 2

A lex was falling! And floating in front of him was his knife! "This is impossible," he blubbered. "How can my knife be in front of me when I'm falling?"

Thinking he was hallucinating, he bit his pinky finger. Immediately, a small trickle of blood emerged. "Where am I going? Oh, this can't be happening!" he screamed. Now he knew, although absurd, that he had fallen through the crazy black hole that his mom had warned him of. His screaming became sobbing. "Mom, where are you?" Alex choked while continuing to descend.

Trying to embolden himself, he reached out and grabbed his knife, hugging it tightly. "Well, no one can get me as long as I have my knife," he thought half-heartedly while looking around, trying to recognize anything normal.

Then as suddenly as his fall had begun, Alex came to a halt. By now, his tears were just about dried up and his throat sore from screaming. He looked around and appeared to be in some kind of cave. But it was a cave like he had never seen before! There were no dark spiders or bats, and it was brightly lit, although he could see no lights, and a green carpet of grass covered all of the immense ground.

Alex inspected himself for injury and was surprised that he could have fallen so far without harm. Pondering his predicament, Alex's fear was rapidly being replaced with curiosity. Enthralled by what was becoming the greatest adventure he had ever experienced, he again scanned the cave.

He slowly stood up, dusted himself off, still ever watchful of his environment. He remembered what his mother had mentioned regarding the "bad." He had no idea of what might constitute any bad anything, and since he wouldn't have believed any of this possible, he was not going to discount any part of her story. Again, he clutched his knife.

Alex started walking. He had no inkling of where to go, and trying to climb out of the cave would have been impossible; he could see the hole that had delivered him, high in the ceiling. *There must be a way to get out of here*, he thought. But how? The grass was soft and felt like a mattress under his feet. It was puzzling. How could such grass as this grow in an underground cave? And where was that light coming from?

Alex continued walking. A patch of darkness caught his eye, and he squinted to ascertain what the shadow might be. Grasping his pen knife as a warrior would a sword, he stepped back. What was it anyway? Whatever it was, it was not moving and was silent.

"Can't sit here forever," he reasoned half-heartedly and continued toward the gloom. As he neared the area, he realized the shadow was not just a patch of darkness but the entrance to a pathway, a trail. Heart beating, he continued. What had he found? Where did it lead to? Fear started to paralyze him; this awful dream/ reality was too much. His knife was a joke. How could he defend himself from the unknown? Again, tears started to well up in his eyes, and he sternly told himself that he was not going to be a sissy.

After all, he had fallen down an impossible deep hole and was still alive.

"Don't be a sissy," he repeated to himself. "I really don't have much choice anyway. I can't fly out of here." He shrugged his shoulders. "This may be a way to get home."

Alex thought of his hero, Genghis Khan. Genghis Khan had been a courageous warrior even though he was a short man. And Alex had read that he had been a brutal soldier. So, he reckoned that if a short, mean warrior could beat armies of thousands as Genghis Khan had, than so could he. Genghis had been an explorer; he had travelled to many foreign lands without the advantage of maps or even GPS. So, with newfound determination, Alex continued toward the trail.

As he neared the entrance, he was relieved to see that it wasn't as dark as it had initially appeared to be. The trail was masked by shadows of giant, leafy trees. Alex walked further into what was now beginning to resemble a jungle. And a dense jungle it was, his pathway almost indistinguishable due to foliage. As he gingerly paced down the trail, he noticed the absence of forest noise—no chirping of birds, no scattering of squirrels, just dead quiet. The first thought that came into his head was the word that his mother had echoed, "bad."

Alex trekked on. Nothing happened. Absolutely nothing. All he could hear was the soft squishing of his feet on the trail. He walked for what seemed like miles but as if in a vacuum. Alex came to a turn in the trail and as he rounded it, he came to a stop. Ahead was a huge building, but it certainly didn't resemble any building that should be in a jungle. It looked more like a temple of some kind.

"What in the heck?" he whispered to himself. Alex immediately thought of the ancient peoples that he had read about in his school-books. Head hunters and sacrifices and real bad juju. He thought it cool when he had read about it then, but it didn't seem so cool now. Alex glanced around, noticing the path that split around this temple building. "Maybe no one is here," he said out loud.

Suddenly, the dismal silence was shattered by a high-pitched screech. Alex screamed and jolted around. There, in the middle of the path that he had just been on, was a creature of the likes he had only read about. Horrified, he stared at the largest bird he had even seen. More so, the "bird" had three heads and claws instead of wings! The clawed nightmare screeched again and jumped forward.

Alex needed no further prompting! Stumbling to his knees, he grabbed dirt and pulled himself up and ahead, never losing sight of the screaming creature behind him. Feeling as if in slow motion, he lurched forward, and this time, his legs came to his rescue. He headed for the entrance of the temple, bounding up the steps three at a time, bursting through the open doorway and behind a statue that stood in the lobby.

Heart pounding and gasping for breath, Alex prayed the monster would not find him. Rattled by what he had just witnessed, he was unsure of what his next move should be. How could he fight off something so terrifying? He had briefly seen some of the creature's capabilities—one head emitting steam from its nose and another spraying streams of orange liquid from its mouth. The screeching was the most baffling as it appeared to emit from a featureless third head with no eyes, ears, or mouth. And where had it come from? Alex had just been on the desolate trail alone just minutes prior.

CHAPTER 3

Alex had to see if the huge creature had followed him. Slowly, he peered from around the statue that he was hiding behind and to his relief, saw nothing. He questioned his mentality. "Am I losing my mind? How could that thing have been right behind me and now it's gone?" he whispered. He reasoned it didn't matter whether it was fictitious in his mind or not; he had seen the creature chase him, and he had felt the heat of the steam it had spewed at him.

Again, he peered from behind the statue. Nothing. With his heartbeat slowing and his breathing becoming normal, Alex felt relief that the threat of the monster, for the moment, seemed to be gone. Alex glanced around the room, wanting to investigate his surroundings. The chamber was large and dark, and it took him a few minutes for his eyes to adjust. As he focused, he was surprised by what he saw. There were numerous statues scattered throughout the room, some resembling the one he had just hidden behind and others that resembled the dragon he was trying to escape from.

Alex hesitantly walked to a dragon statue. It resembled a toad with a dog's body. Its eyes were huge, and its mouth seemed to grin. Its feet had large, black claws on them, and the tail was long and slithery. It was scary, and it was ugly. Unable to look at it any longer, he turned to investigate the others.

Alex was surprised that there were statues that actually looked normal. In a corner of the room stood a life-sized statue of a buck and a doe deer. They looked out of place amidst the abominations surrounding them. Alex felt a sense of peace as he inspected them. They were detailed in every way; he could even see the eye lashes of the doe's soft, kind face. As he stared, he felt himself slipping into a dreamlike state. Not having the strength to will himself to stop, he found himself in a valley of grandiose beauty, grass greener than any he had ever seen, the cloudless sky a blend of blue and pink ribbon that extended as far as his eyes could see. He saw giant trees, easily four times the size of redwoods he had seen in pictures. Everywhere there was life, small animals scampering around and birds, many of which he had never seen before, flying their ballet in the sky.

Alex felt a joy and energy he had never before experienced, not even at Christmas. He wanted to stay in this valley and never leave, knowing he would be safe and happy. Glancing around, he was elated to see cows and horses grazing peacefully. Alex could not contain the smile that spread across his face as, upon closer inspection, he discovered the horses were in actuality, grazing unicorns! They were the most beautiful creatures he had ever seen; patterns of black and white speckled their coats, manes, and tails, while enormous wings of gold and silver adorned their backs. He found their physical beauty mesmerizing, and he could somehow feel their love for him. Then, as suddenly as the daydream had begun, it was over.

Startled, Alex awoke to find himself staring at the delicate doe statue. He was still in the "statue room," as he had come to call it. Perplexed, he sat on a stone bench near the doe. "What is happening to me?" he said. "This place is too much, too weird, and I need to get home before I lose all my marbles."

Glancing around, he noticed several more statues of a more normal kind. Two stately lions reminded him of the pair that guarded the entrance to the downtown library. "Pretty typical," he mentioned as he studied them. He lingered a moment and then moved on. The remaining statues were unremarkable, a few Cupid-type angels and several more gargoyles. Not knowing what may lay in wait, Alex pressed on. But where to? He walked to the entrance of the temple and cautiously peeked around. Nothing was there. He wished for the sounds of life that he had heard while in his trance. Alex now knew that just because something seemed so in this place did not mean it was so. He had mistakenly presumed earlier that a silent jungle meant a peaceful jungle. He would have to be more careful as life in this world did not follow the patterns of the world he had left. He turned and looked at the doe still standing peacefully next to the buck. He felt so safe being near her. Sighing, he turned again and started for the entrance.

Alex walked out the door and stopped. Scrutinizing all directions, he slowly started down the steps, knowing that he could immediately retrace his steps back into the safety of the temple if need be.

CHAPTER 4

"**D**on't be afraid. I will be watching over you**.**"

Alex gasped and turned in an instant. "Who's there?" he hissed, fear overcoming him. Grasping his knife, Alex repeated. "Who's there?" while turning in a quick circle and trying to sound brave. When no answer followed, he crept down a few more stairs and stopped. "For Pete's sake, now I'm hearing voices."

The temple was seated in the bifurcation of the roads, and Alex had no idea of which to follow; both were unmarked, looked identical, and led into the jungle. Just as a tear started to form, the Voice again erupted, **"Take the path that leads to the right."**

Feeling terrified yet somehow knowing that the Voice meant him no harm, Alex answered sheepishly, "OK." He again viewed the area immediately around him and saw nothing. Alex had heard of mental telepathy; he knew that there were folks who somehow could transmit their thoughts as he had seen it in some movies. But he couldn't imagine that he could actually transmit his thoughts to a person or animal. He felt terrified of a voice he could not see but realized that he had no power over it, and so he calmed himself to continue.

Redirecting himself, he started down the path that led to the right. He glanced at his watch. "Five o'clock!" he gasped. "That can't be possible. I fell down that hole around ten a.m. There's no way that I've been down here for that long!" He looked at his watch again. All of the parts seemed to be working; even the glow in the dark was alit. How could the time have escaped him? Had he been asleep and not known or in an altered state whilst in the daydream?

Alex felt the urge to get moving. Not knowing if this strange world had regular daytime and nighttime, he didn't want to chance being left out in the unknown night. And he felt hungry! "No wonder my belly's growling," he said while shaking his head. "It's been a long time since breakfast. What am I going to eat?" he asked himself. He waited a moment, hoping the Voice would chirp up and tell him that there was a Burger King around the bend!

"What a nerd I am!" he giggled. "Yeah, sure, a Burger King in the middle of a dream jungle! Heck, I bet it even has a drive-up window or fly-up window depending on if you are a dragon or not!"

Alex spotted a large rock on the edge of the path and sat on it. *Crunch!* He jumped up, reached into the back pocket of his jeans, and pulled out the semi-squashed Crispy Way bar that he had stashed there earlier that morning. Hungrily, he tore it open and demolished it. It was delicious! But no sooner had he taken the last bite that he immediately felt remorse. "What did I just do?" he said aloud. "Man, I should have saved some of that candy bar! What if there isn't anything for me to eat here? Well, dumb me! Too late now!"

Resolving to try and plan better, he started walking again. Feeling stronger after eating, his step quickened. He soon found himself running down the path, never, ever having had this much energy from one candy bar. It felt great!

Caution! flashed in his mind, scolding him that he should be more careful and take discretion on this journey. But at that moment, Alex could have cared less. He felt as if he could fly; he wanted to fly! He ran faster, sampling the fragrances around him and laughing aloud. This place was beautiful, and he never wanted to leave! The trees were larger than he had ever seen, the leaves so huge that he could lie upon them! He thought he could hear sweet music in the distance, and so, he ran faster. He could not believe that his legs could run so fast and not tire.

The music became louder now, a sweet blend of voices and heavenly orchestra, and he wanted to be in the middle of it all— immediately! Shocking himself, Alex shouted aloud, "Well, I'll just fly there!" Immediately, he felt himself leave the path and become airborne! His joy uncontained, he rose higher and higher, amazed and overwhelmed at the indescribable beauty of the scenery below him yet not curious as to how he could actually be flying. Colors blended from every rainbow imaginable; land and sky became one, and Alex thought this must be the way angels lived every day.

Maybe I'm dead and an angel, he thought. *Maybe that dragon really did kill me, and I just don't know it yet.* Alex brought his finger to his mouth and bit it hard. Ouch, it hurt! "Guess I'm not dead then," he said. "Angels don't bleed, and boy, this sucker is bleeding bad." He sucked on the wound for a moment and stared at it. This was really happening! He couldn't help but wonder what his buddies back at home would make of all this.

Alex flew on, following the music, which now seemed to be fading. He flew over land and forest for what seemed to be forever when suddenly, up ahead, he saw a huge building. "Wonder what that is?" he muttered. "Sure didn't notice that before."

As he continued to fly toward it, the beautiful music that had been dimming now became loud and delightful. Alex's head was spinning; the combination of the grandeur of what now looked like a castle and the heavenly music was just too much! "Bad anything, my eye!" he whispered. This was beyond anything in his wildest dreams! He directed his flight down, determined to land on the outskirts of the castle until he learned more about it.

The landing was smooth and easy. Alex turned and stared at the impressive structure. *Wonder who lives here?* he thought.

"Beware!" a voice shouted into his mind. **"Things are not as they seem."** The Voice! It was back!

"What do you mean beware?" Alex asked. "This place is beautiful, and maybe someone here knows how I can get back home."

"Beware, Alex, things are not as they seem," the Voice restated.

Alex sat down. He was really confused now. The grass felt like velvet, and it was beyond beautiful. Flowers exploded from all around him, singing sweet, lilting tunes as they swayed in the soft breeze. The castle loomed in front of him with majesty and power he had never before experienced. And to top it all off, Alex had actually flown! Not walked but flown, and on his own command! But now the Voice sounded urgent and had addressed him by name, which it hadn't done before.

Alex's euphoria vanished. "Why don't you tell me who you are and why you are following me? And if you're so worried about me, then why don't you take me home?"

The Voice continued, **"Alex, I am your friend. Soon you will know who I am. I care about you, but I can only do so much at this time. I cannot take you to your home, but I can help you get there. You must believe me that there is danger here, but you will still need to go to the castle. It will be a means to help you get home. Be mindful and watchful of all around you and take nothing at face value. There is bad here, but there is also good. You will have to decide which is which; I cannot help you to determine that either. But I can help you in many ways that you will soon see. Follow your heart—it will lead you to the good,**

which you will need to get home. The bad knows you are here and will try to obstruct your safe return."

Now Alex was blown away. "The bad knows I'm here?" he retorted. "You have got to tell me what it looks like. How am I gonna fight bad whatever it is with a knife? Oh, this is great. You are my friend, but I can't see you and, actually, can't even hear you except in my head, which I think I'm really losing now. What am I gonna do?" Alex started to cry. "At least Genghis Khan could see his enemies," he said in between sobs.

The Voice tried to soothe him. **"I've already told you what I can. In time, you will see me. You are not crazy, Alex. I think you are a very brave boy. Remember what I've told you, and you will be safe. You are a good boy, and that will help to keep the bad at bay for a while."**

Alex listened to every word the Voice had to say to him. He fervently wished his mother was here to protect him. "What should I do now?" he asked.

"Go to the castle. There is an old man who lives there. His name is Quinn, and he can help you. But beware! Although the castle looks to be close by, it is still far away. Remember, things are not as they seem. Be careful on your journey there. The path is well-marked, but the dangers that lurk in it are not. I will be watching over you and will help when I can. Go now."

Alex waited for more but there was complete silence.

"What do I do when I get there? What do I say to the old man?" Alex again waited. Nothing. He repeated himself urgently. Still nothing. Finding a Kleenex in his pocket (funny, he didn't recall placing it there earlier), Alex wiped his eyes and blew his nose. Feeling much older and more tired than a ten-year-old should, he sat on the grass. "I'm getting tired of this bad or good dream or whatever it is," he said. "I want to go home."

Knowing in his heart that what the Voice had told him was true, he resolved to get moving. He had so many questions and no answers to any of them. "But if I've made it this far and I'm not dead, then I guess I can get through the rest of it," he reasoned. Of course, he had no clue what the "rest of it" might be. Turning toward the direction of the castle, he started to walk. Again, he could hear the "angel music," but it had faded. The energy he had felt earlier was now replaced with bone-weary fatigue.

CHAPTER 5

Alex walked toward the majestic structure. It was just like the pictures he had seen of old European castles but with a hint of the supernatural. It reminded him of a combination of the Dark Ages and Disney World, kind of like Cinderella's castle with a twist. The Voice had been right; the castle was not as close as it appeared to be. "Well," Alex said to himself, "That seems to be the norm around here." He continued on, wary eyes on the alert. Nothing had changed. He was now on the outskirts of the jungle, the perimeter of thousands of acres of lush, green grass and wild-flowers. The meadow seemed to give him a jump start.

The grass was up to his knees, and he waded in bountiful, col-orful flowers from his ankles to the top of his head. It reminded him of the preview to the old *Little House on the Prairie* reruns, where Laura and her sisters ran through the pasture of wildflowers. He was breathless. The fragrance of the field was overpowering. He was surprised by his attention and reaction to what he had previously regarded as "girly stuff." He was glad that none of his buddies were here to see him so emotional.

Unable to explain his newfound sensitivity, he threw himself full force into the joy of the meadow. Alex's exhaustion quickly gave way to boundless energy. Running through the meadow, he could hardly contain the joy he felt and began to laugh aloud. On and on he ran, his legs a never-ending powerhouse. The flowers' scents seemed to boost him on. He actually thought he could hear them singing, the sound similar to the angel music he had heard earlier. The further he ran, the louder the music; it was as if it surrounded him. Flowers singing—this place made Disney World obsolete! He didn't care if it was the flowers or the trees or whatever it was that made the music; he didn't want it to ever end.

Alex stopped. He wasn't tired. He still felt as though he could run forever. But he could see that he was nearing the castle and needed to be alert, remembering what the Voice had warned him numerous times about. Now the music had dimmed to an almost background sound; it was as if the flowers knew that he needed to concentrate on his surroundings.

Alex was close enough now to see the trim on the castle walls. Several of the windows were decorated with hideous gargoyles, miniature replicas of the ones Alex had seen in the temple. Other windows were obscured by massive, clingy vines that grew up its solid walls. Alex thought that from this point, the castle was more like the Dark Ages and definitely not Cinderella's castle. He quietly advanced toward the ominous building. "Why would such an ugly castle be in the middle of such a beautiful field?" he asked aloud. Although he still felt energized, he felt uneasy and proceeded with caution. He was still puzzled as to the absence of wildlife in the magnificent field. "I have to remember what my friend the Voice told me," he muttered and continued to walk.

Now Alex could see the artistry on the castle walls. Engravings of elfin pixies decorated the front wall, and creatures he had never seen before snaked around the corners. It was beautiful but eerie. "I don't know if I really wanna go in there," he murmured. "This place is kinda scary." Scary, yes, but still exciting! He didn't know if any of his friends had ever been to a real castle, and here he was about to enter a real (or was it?) one. He wished he had a camera to prove to his buddies that this place really existed. The surrounding grounds were as breathtakingly beautiful as the castle was ugly. Flower gardens were scattered in patterns that magnified the colors within them. He expected thousands of butterflies and birds to emerge at any time, but still the area was without life.

Suddenly the path ended. What was this? Wow, a moat! He hadn't noticed this from where he had been standing a few moments ago. "Now, how am I gonna get across this?" he wondered. He decided not to try to swim it; it was large, at least fifty feet wide, and he had no idea how deep it could be. Nor did he have an inkling what might be in it. Normal fish or alligators would be dangerous enough, and he doubted that there would be anything normal in these waters. "This is gonna be hard," Alex said as he looked around for a much-needed bridge or stairwell across the water.

"Walk around the castle but beware. What you need is not far." The Voice! It was back!

"Which way do I walk?" Alex asked aloud. Again, the Voice repeated the same message. "Ok, ok," retorted Alex, slightly irritated. He wanted the Voice to just talk to him like a normal person, omitting the riddles. He walked on and came upon a well-worn path that ran next to the moat. After walking for about ten minutes, he noticed what appeared to be a boat on the shoreline. The Voice had been right! Alex ran to it, then screeched to a stop. Something was weird here. The boat secured to the edge of the moat looked just like a toy boat that he used to have! Alex blinked. Perhaps his eyes were playing tricks on him.

"Maybe this boat was the model that all the toy boats were made from," he reasoned. He walked up to the boat and stooped to inspect it closer. To his amazement, the boat was identical to the toy he had owned. How could this be? This boat had the same bright red body with the green trim, and it had oars just like his old one. Alex hadn't seen his boat in a long time; it had been stashed under his bed with a ton of other broken toys. His boat had a crack in its bow, and his mom had vowed to trash any broken toys, so Alex had shoved it to the back of the pack, hoping she wouldn't find it. With time, he had forgotten about it entirely.

Alex looked again at the life-sized replica of his toy. Then he saw it—the crack! There was a crack in the bow of this boat, just like the one that his toy had. Alex had believed that he couldn't be surprised in this strange land anymore. And again, he had been proven wrong. He sat and stared at the boat. "I wonder how it got here? This is crazy. There is no way that a toy that has been under my bed could be in this place now. I'm goin nuts!"

Alex reached out and touched the boat. He felt the wood and knocked on the hull and heard its hollow echo. "So much for my goin nuts," Alex said. "This is my old boat, and I guess it's here for a reason. Hmm, I wonder if it will float with me in it?" Alex looked into the boat. It was dry. He remembered that his toy boat still raced in the bathtub, even with a crack in it. He reasoned that if it worked in his tub then it would probably work here too.

Slowly, Alex shoved the boat off the slant of the moat wall. He let it out about four feet and watched for telltale signs of water leakage. There were none. Alex pulled the boat back to the bank and climbed in. "Well, here goes nothing," he muttered. "Sure hope I don't end up some monster's snack!" Wrapping the rope tether into a neat pile, he grabbed both oars and started to paddle toward the castle.

No monsters appeared in the water. Grateful that the boat was seaworthy, he rowed on. Closer and closer the castle loomed. Afraid that something would happen, Alex rowed for all he was worth. A flicker caught the corner of his eye. What was that? A glimmer of light on the waves he made with every stroke of his oars? There it was again! Faster he rowed; twenty feet, now ten feet left to go. Alex momentarily glanced into the water, trying to see what was causing the glittering light. He immediately became transfixed, now leaving the boat and entering the water. It was similar to the feeling he had experienced when he had encountered the doe in the temple. Alex thought he should be scared, but oddly enough, he felt no fear, only peace and happiness. He was amazed that he could see clearly and breathe easily while under the water. He scanned the area. Millions of brilliant-colored fish mingled around him and seemed to delight in his presence.

Alex swam with them and explored the depths of the water. In and out of caverns they journeyed. The water world was a child's delight; porpoises cavorted with him, and he stowed a ride on several. Knowing that it was not usual to find porpoises or caverns in a moat didn't dull his excitement at all. Alex swam past swaying underwater forests of vegetation, and he laughed aloud for the joy of this world. Just to be able to laugh underwater was a hoot! He continued to swim, buoyed on by his newfound independence.

"Stop!"

Alex's swimming came to a halt. "What was that?" he said. Then he heard it again.

"Stop!"

He looked around. Nothing but fish. "Is that you, Voice?" Alex asked.

"Do not go any further. There is danger ahead!"

The dream trance ended as suddenly as it had begun. Alex found himself back in the boat, staring into the water. "What's goin on here?" he asked. "What happened?" he repeated.

"Get to the castle now!" The Voice was loud and urgent. Alex didn't need a second prompting. Grabbing the oars, he rowed for all he was worth. He could see the opposite shore only a few feet away. He rammed the boat's bow into the sand and quickly leaped out of it. Just as his feet hit the ground, he heard a deafening roar behind him.

Terrified, he turned to see a serpent the size of a house right on his tail. The monster was black and purple and had orange eyes that had pupils of coal. It reared its ugly head and spit what appeared to be liquid fire at him. Alex couldn't believe his eyes. Where had this thing come from? He had just been "in the water" (although he wasn't wet at all), and all he had seen was beauty. If he hadn't been warned, he would have ended up as the "monster snack" he had joked about earlier.

Alex squirmed up the bank of the moat in reverse, his eyes never leaving the hideous thing that continued to advance toward him. "Get away from me!" he screamed. The sea creature continued to advance, hissing and spitting wet fire. Did it come out of the water? Alex didn't think so. He had never heard of sea monsters that could walk on land, but then again, he had never heard of sea monsters living in a moat alongside porpoises and ocean fish!

Still retreating, Alex grabbed a handful of dirt and threw it at the oncoming nightmare. The thing screeched and backed up. Was the monster afraid of dirt? Feeling his confidence grow, Alex used both hands, dug in, and threw shore dirt as fast as he could. The serpent continued to screech and wail its displeasure at the dirt shower and then slowly started to retreat, emitting a final bellow and dipping under the water's surface. And Alex, crawling backwards, found himself at the crest of the moat wall.

Trying to catch his breath, he fell onto his back and started to cry. Was this ever going to end? Would he ever get home? It seemed for every happy adventure he experienced, there was a horrible one awaiting him. He lay a few minutes and rested, feeling exhausted and hungry. Alex glanced at his watch. It was 9:00 p.m.—no wonder he was tired! He looked around and noticed the daylight waning.

He needed somewhere to rest safely for the night. The castle was a stone's throw away and offered him a place of refuge, despite its threatening appearance. Alex trudged up the slight incline to a large wooden door. What to do? He hesitated to knock on it.

Looking around, he noted a smaller door further down the castle wall. Maybe he could sneak into the structure and rest and then try to find the old man later. Alex walked to the small door, and he immediately thought of the tiny door that Alice had found in the story *Alice in Wonderland.* He tried the knob and to his surprise was able to easily open it. *Almost too easy,* he thought. Slowly, he pushed the door open and peered in.

The room was dark, so he opened the door further to inspect it. A small table sat in the center of it and on it, a large basket of fruit and bread. It looked delicious, and Alex was famished. Caution being thrown to the wind, he tackled the food. Attacking the apples and bananas, he then downed a large breadstick. The food all looked and tasted normal. As he ate, he inspected the room. An overstuffed bed occupied a corner; a wooden cabinet faced the bed on the opposite wall and next to that sat a small table with a wooden basin with water and brightly colored towels. Ignoring the convenience of the situation, he immediately made himself at home. A small lantern sat on the table, and he lit it with some matches that were neatly placed next to it. He walked over to the basin and proceeded to wash up. Whereas at home, his mother couldn't get him near the bathtub, he now scrubbed the layers of dirt that had accumulated throughout the day.

Feeling refreshed after the food and bath, he continued to explore the room. Curious as to the contents of the large cabinet, Alex opened the wooden door. Much to his surprise, he found a clean pair of pants and a clean shirt hanging in it. Stranger still, the clothing looked to be his size. His present clothing in shambles from the adventures of the day, Alex quickly put the clean clothes on.

They fit! They weren't anything he would want to wear to school, but they were clean and dry and felt wonderful.

Alex opened a drawer. A belt lay in it, and he picked it up and placed it around his waist. It also fit. He opened another drawer and this time found a pair of shoes. The shoes were really some kind of boots, but they were dry and obviously new. He knew the boots would fit, and he eagerly put them on. One more drawer yielded a sweater-type jacket, and Alex removed it. He held it up and eyeballed its size. He walked over to the bed and sat on it. He placed the jacket on the bedpost and lay back on the bed. Boy, did it feel great! The blanket was plush and heavy, and the pillow looked to be made of goose down. Not having the will to get up, Alex immediately fell asleep. According to his watch, it was now 11:00 p.m.

CHAPTER 6

The next morning (at least he thought it was morning; he wasn't sure that there had even been a night), Alex awoke with a start. Transiently confused as to where he was and what time it was, he checked his watch. It was nine o'clock! He had slept ten hours! He couldn't believe it. Everything was as he had left it. Alex felt refreshed and rested. Remembering the food in the bowl, he got up and reached for a banana. Downing that in record time, he finished off the remaining breadsticks and apples. Wanting to rinse his face, he was surprised to find fresh water in the bowl on the table and proceeded to wash up. Not one to question oddity in this place anymore, he dried off, retrieved his clothing, and finished dressing. With that done, Alex scanned the room again. He had wanted to explore it further last night but had fallen asleep. Not noting anything more of interest, he walked to the door and opened it. The sun was shining, and there was a warm breeze. He closed the door and went back to sit on the bed. "What do I do next?" he pondered.

"Look around you, Alex." The Voice! It was back again! Alex was reassured and felt comfort when he heard his invisible friend's kind voice.

Alex answered, "Look for what? Do you know whose room this is? Where do I go now to find the old man?"

"One thing at a time, Alex. Look around the room. You will find a door that leads into the castle. Find the door and follow your heart. You will find the old man. But beware for there is danger in the castle, too. I will watch over you. Be careful."

"Where are you? Where's the door? Why can't you just show me where it is? Please talk to me. Whose room is this?" Alex's words tumbled out as fast as he thought of them.

But there was no answer. The room was still.

Alex kicked out at nothing. "Why does the old Voice play games with me? He always says what he wants to say but never answers my questions or just talks with me. Oh, whatever! I'm not gonna get bent outta shape about it. I've got to find that door. If the Voice says it's here, then it's here."

Alex climbed off the bed and started to look around. The back of the room was dark, so he grabbed the lantern off the table and started to walk. As he neared the rear of the room, he was surprised to see what appeared to be the outline of a door. It was merged with the rock wall, and Alex wondered if it had been a secret entry to a disguised passage. He looked for a doorknob, but there was none. "How am I gonna open this without a doorknob?" Alex said frustrated.

Alex pushed on a corner of the door, and surprisingly, the border gave way, opening into a candlelit hallway. Grasping his pocketknife, he took a deep breath and proceeded through the door. The hall was musty and damp, and he stifled a sneeze. Wanting to keep his arrival unannounced for as long as possible, he crept slowly, ever vigilant of his surroundings.

On and on he tread without any interruptions or any life noted, besides himself. Then as suddenly as he started, he found himself at the end of the hall, which bifurcated into two longer hallways. *Which way?* he thought, hoping now that the Voice would come to his aid. Again, total quiet. "What the heck?" he snorted. Tossing care to the wind, he veered left. This new hall was identical to the one he had just left, stone and candles. Alex was desperate to find an exit from the overall gloomy state that surrounded him, gargoyle-like statues and winged spiders. He wished that the gentle doe that he had seen earlier in his journey would be present to give him a sense of peace and safety.

Alex hadn't traversed a hundred feet when he heard a loud boom! He jumped backwards and landed on the floor, straining to determine the direction of what sounded like a very loud drumbeat while trying to keep his heartbeat in his chest. Terrified, he crawled to his knees and slowly stood up.

Boom! Boom! Boom! The beats continued their rhythmic procession, which sounded to be heading straight to where he stood. Alex didn't know what to do. There was no place to hide in this hallway. Recalling that the hall had divided into two directions, he turned and retreated back the way he had previously come from. Within minutes, he was back at the junction of the halls. He continued to run. Finally, he slowed to a jog while intermittently glancing over his shoulder, then came to a halt. He could still hear the drums, but they sounded distant now. Alex thought that was weird as moments ago, the banging had sounded to be right behind him.

Alex scanned the hallway again. He noticed a light further down the hall and headed toward it, hoping it might be a place of refuge. Resuming his jog, he noticed doorways scattered to the right and left of him. He stopped and tried the first door to his right. It was locked. He ran across the hall and tried a door on his left. Ugh, it was also locked. "Great," he muttered. The drumbeat advanced again toward him at a steady pace. Alex started to jog again, trying all doors only to find them all locked. Now panicked, he tried a final door to his right and gave it a half-hearted turn. It opened! Delighted but stunned, Alex entered the room and shut the door. The room was lit by several lanterns and many smaller candles. Except for the wooden furniture in it, it was empty.

"Anyone here?" Alex asked in a subdued voice. No answer. He repeated the question. Still no answer. He inspected the room again. It was almost identical to the one he had stayed in last night. He noticed a latch on the door and locked it. The drumming advanced and now sounded to be right outside the door! His heart pounding, he was unsure of what to expect if the drummer or whatever it was tried to enter the room. Alex felt desperate, checking the wall, hoping to find another secret door like he had found before. No door. Alex was confused. It seemed as though this drummer knew exactly where he was no matter where he tried to hide, and now the drumming was so loud it was causing the floor to vibrate. *That drum has got to be huge to shake a floor like this*, he thought. Louder and louder the sound became until the lantern shook and Alex had to grab it for fear it would fall off the table.

Then suddenly as it had started, the drumming stopped. Alex's eyes widened, and a lump formed in his throat. He listened for footsteps or anything that might indicate what could be lurking outside his door.

Tap! Tap! Tap!

Alex froze. The knocking continued.

"Alex, are you in there?" asked an unfamiliar voice. "Please open the door. I need to take you to the king."

Alex felt faint. The drummer knew who he was!

"Who are you?" he asked. "What king are you talking about?"

The voice answered. "My name is Po. The king knows you are here. He knew you were here last night too; we all did. But we knew you were tired, so we let you rest. He wants to talk with you, and he sent me to get you. Don't be afraid. I won't hurt you, and neither will the king."

Alex continued, "Why did you beat the drums and scare me instead of just coming to get me?" He tried to peek through the keyhole to see Po, but it was too small.

Po answered, "I always beat the drum. It's my job. I beat the drum for the king. So when he asked me to come and get you, I beat my drum because it is an honor to please him. I'm sorry if I scared you."

Alex unlatched the door and inched it open.

"Hello," said Po.

Standing in front of the door was a young boy about Alex's age, holding a large drum. The drum was secured by a strap around his neck, and Alex wondered how he could hold it up. Po was smiling and held out his hand.

Alex opened the door a little more and looked at him. "Hi," he said. "My name is Alex."

"I know," laughed Po. "Like I said, we knew you were here."

Alex looked at Po. Something was different about him. He looked at him closer and realized that Po resembled a toy that he had once had, a doll that had been given to him when he was very young. He hadn't seen the doll in a very long time and had figured his mom had thrown it out during one of her cleaning binges. "You look familiar to me," Alex said to the boy.

"I should," said Po, "I was once under your bed. Do you remember the doll that you got for Christmas a long time ago? You used to call me Pooh! Your mom used to laugh when you called me that; she told you that there was a bear named Pooh, not a little boy!"

"Wait a minute. You're telling me that you were once a toy that I used to have and that you were under my bed? Is this a dream within a dream? Who are you really? I know that dolls don't come to life, not even in this weird place."

"Yes, Alex, I am that doll. But I am alive and have been for a long time. It is no dream, see?" And with that, he touched Alex's arm.

"No!" Alex jumped back.

Po laughed. "I'm not going to hurt you. I'm going to try to help you! You want to go home, right?"

Now Alex was all ears. The door was wide open, and Po entered the room.

"I saw you when you rowed across the moat. I was worried about you because the moat is enchanted, and there are many who haven't made it across it because of the sea monster. You saw him, right?"

Alex nodded his head. Po continued, "You were lucky. Most folks go into the trance and end up as monster snacks. What woke you up?" Po asked.

"The Voice told me to run!" said Alex. Po and Alex sat on the bed and continued their conversation.

"What voice was that?" asked Po.

"I don't know who it is," replied Alex. "But he is always there when I need him or at least, most of the time. I started hearing him after I had the dream at the temple," Alex continued.

"What dream are you talking about?" Po asked. "Are you talking about the temple in the jungle?"

"Wow, you mean you know what I'm talking about? The old temple in the forest that has all the statues in it? I had a dream when I was looking at one of the statues. It was so neat! I could fly and do whatever I wanted! I felt happy and not scared. I thought that that must be what heaven must be like."

Po looked thoughtfully at Alex. "Someone is watching over you. I can't believe that you even made it to the temple; all the others haven't. Did you see anything before you entered it?"

"Wow, did I see anything? Not much, except a huge dragon that chased me into a room in the temple! It was the scariest thing I have ever seen. It had three heads, and one of the heads had no eyes, nose, or mouth but kept screeching at me. I thought I was gonna die! I ran into the temple and hid behind a statue. Boy, some of those statues were pretty scary too. But there was one, a statue of a doe deer, and she wasn't scary. And this may sound stupid, but I felt safe around her. It was when I was looking at her that I had the dream."

Po was solemn. "My friend, you are blessed. That dragon is a demon from beyond, and he guards that temple. The temple used to be a sacred place; the statues that scared you were placed there to ward off anyone like yourself. The doe that you describe was not there the last time I was there, but she must have been placed there for a reason. Perhaps the voice that you heard is the voice of that sweet doe. Anyway, the fact that you made it past the dragon is nothing short of a miracle. There is a reason that you are here."

Alex continued with his questions. "Was that your room that I stayed in last night? How can you help me to get back home?" Alex was getting excited, and Po was in wonderment over the narrow escapes of his newfound friend. "Po, can you hear me?" urged Alex.

Po woke up. "Oh, I'm sorry. I just can't believe that you have journeyed so far and have been so protected. Anyway, I'm glad that you are here. We have a lot to do. Now, what was your question? About the room? Yes, that is my room, and I was glad to share it with you. The clothes were mine also, and I was happy to give them to you. Now we must go and find the king; he wants to speak with you. He is a good man but a little odd at times. Finding goodness in this land is a blessing for there is much that is not good here. We are somewhat safe in this castle, but we still need to be careful for it has happened before that the evil has crept through the walls. I believe the evil knows you are here and will try anything to get to you. You see, you've escaped it, and it is not used to having anyone do that. It will be very angry. So come on, and we will find the king."

Po extended his hand. Alex had a million questions to ask but was tired of talking. He nodded his head and took Po's hand. Po picked up his drum, and they started out the door and down the hall. The drum was silent now. It was as if Po knew that Alex needed some time to digest all that he had heard. Further down the hall they walked, twisting and turning in silence.

As they walked, Alex noticed that the hallway had become lighter; there were tapestries and paintings that adorned the walls with brilliant color and replaced the prior dismal conditions. He broke the silence. "Are we almost there?" he asked.

"Yes, we only have a little further to go," replied Po.

Alex continued to think. How could this be? He was talking to a previous toy of his and had befriended him. And now he was walking through a castle and depending on a toy and a king that he had never seen before to help him. How much stranger could this adventure get? He shuddered to think. He knew that Po was impressed with his narrow escapes from monsters that shouldn't even exist. Why had he been spared? Alex knew the Voice had played a key role in this drama, but he still didn't know why or what his part would be. Could the Voice really be that deer back at the temple? Or was she something else? Perhaps it wasn't the doe but the stag instead? Alex didn't know.

A thought popped into his mind suggesting that perhaps it was his father. He knew it was a crazy notion as his father had been dead for many years. He barely remembered him, but his mother had explained that although his dad hadn't had much time with him, he had loved Alex with all his heart and would for all eternity. Those kind words had comforted him whenever he felt lonely for his dad; it was hard at times watching his buddies hang out with their fathers. He was grateful that he was often included in activities with his friends and their dads. As much as he loved his mother, she just wasn't into fishing or camping.

Po stopped at a large door. "Ok, Alex, we're here. This is the king's chamber. Just knock and enter. I'll see you later."

"Wait a minute!" Alex shouted. "I can't go in there by myself. I don't even know this guy. I know he's a king, but I don't want to go in there alone. Please come with me. He wouldn't mind, would he? Please?"

"I think the king wanted to see you alone, Alex," Po replied. "But I guess it wouldn't hurt if I went in with you. We're friends, right? You really loved me when you were little," Po smiled. "But you have to knock."

Alex knocked on the door.

"Enter," a voice replied. Alex cautiously opened the door.

"Please come in, my boy," the voice continued.

Alex and Po walked through the door and entered a huge room. It was bright and airy; large open windows drowning the room in brilliant sunshine and scented breezes. Flowers and green and pink plants adorned the numerous wooden tables and cabinets. Alex expected fairies to pop out at any moment!

"Welcome."

Alex turned in the direction of the voice and stared. Sitting on a throne of blended silver and gold sat the most impressive man Alex had ever seen.

"I am King Quinn," he said, his voice deep and strong yet kind. "I have been waiting for you. Do not be afraid. I will not hurt you."

The king smiled and held out his hand as if to shake Alex's. Alex looked at Po. Po nodded.

Alex walked toward the king, extending his hand in greeting. The king's grip was firm but gentle. He inspected the old man— long, flowing white hair that framed gentle blue eyes and a rounded, kindly face. His tall and somewhat stocky frame was draped in a burgundy and silver floor-length robe, reflecting strength yet patience and love. Alex immediately relaxed and smiled. He felt safe and secure in this man's presence.

The king continued, "I know you must have many questions. Perhaps I can help to answer them. You are quite a boy, Alex. Po tells me that you made it past the temple dragon and the serpent in the moat. Not many are able to do that. You must be very special." The king stood as he talked to Alex.

"Yes, sir, but I have a lot of questions. Those monsters scared me half to death. Why are those creatures even here? Are there more? Can you tell me where I am and how I can get back home? My mom must be crazy with worry by now! She doesn't know where I am."

"Whoa, lad, slow down! I am king but can still only answer one question at a time! Ok, first question." The king walked to his throne and sat. "Come and sit, Alex. We have much to discuss."

Alex walked to the cushioned chair that the king pointed at and sat.

"I know you must be hungry and thirsty. I will have food and drink brought to you." The king glanced at Po. Po nodded and left the room. Alex immediately felt embarrassed as he had totally forgotten his friend's presence.

"Don't worry about Po," the king said. "He has his job to do, and he understands. You will see him again. Now, back to the many questions you have. You are in a special land, Alex. Most people do not know that it even exists, and I doubt that many would believe it even if they were aware. This land has been here forever; it was here before I became king, and I have been here a very long time. It is a land of good and also of bad. I believe that you have seen some of the bad, am I correct?"

Alex nodded his head.

The king continued. "We have a fair amount of visitors here, and they are of all ages. Most of the time they are children, like yourself. Very rarely do we have an adult visit. Anyway, this ancient land is very different from your world. You noticed that Po looked familiar to you, did you not? I know you must have been surprised when he told you that he had been a favorite toy of yours. And I know that you must be curious as to how and why he is here, just like I'm sure that you would like to know the same regarding yourself."

Alex was all ears. All he could do was nod.

CHAPTER 7

The king continued. "This land is called Jin, and it is between your world and many others. The God who created your world also created this one. He is the most kind, loving God. This is a world for things that no one wants anymore, whether it be people or items. The rules for life in your world do not apply here. You would never see a doll walk and talk in your world, but it is the norm here. Did Po tell you how he came to be here?"

Alex shook his head.

The king resumed. "Po fell down the hole under your bed." Quinn waited to see Alex's reaction. All of Alex's attention was focused on the king, and he anxiously awaited every word.

"I expect the space under your bed was not the cleanest nor the tidiest area of your bedroom."

Again, Alex nodded. "It wasn't. My mom said it was a pigsty."

The king smiled. "That's the usual situation here. All the people, the animals, and toys that come here are from areas just like that under your bed. When it gets too crowded, then they fall into the hole and end up here. Most of the time, the ones that come here are glad they did for they were not loved or cared for anymore in their old home. It doesn't mean that they were not previously. Often, they just get replaced by something newer or their owner has lost interest in them. Then, once in a while, we find a little boy like yourself. You fell down a hole under your bed, didn't you, Alex?"

"Yes, sir, I did. My mom tried to tell me about the black hole under my bed and about the bad and good whatever. She never told me what the bad and good meant. I laughed at her and was mad because she wouldn't let me go out to play. I thought that she had made it all up to get me to clean my room. I guess she was telling me the truth."

"She sure was, Alex," Quinn remarked. "And I'm sure that you do not want to stay here forever, right?"

The thought of staying in this forbidding but exciting place made Alex shudder. "No, sir," he replied.

"Your mother was right about the good and the bad here. I don't know how she knew about us, but someone must have told her at some time. I do remember that long ago, there was a little girl who visited us, but she didn't stay long. She was very sweet, and we were worried that the monsters of the bad would get to her. They didn't. Just like they didn't get to you. I think both of you have something special. Anyway, I will help you to get back home, but it will take hard work, and some of the journey is not without danger. The way that brought you to the castle is not the same route that will get you home. In other words, you cannot retrace your steps to get to where you first came. Do you remember the cave?"

Alex nodded.

"Well, you will have to travel to another area similar to the cave, but you will take a different route. I will send Po with you so that you will not be alone. He will be able to help, but most of the journey will be up to you. Jin is a beautiful land, but as I have said, not without many dangers. It was not always this way."

"You see, many years ago, there was a ruler, and he was all powerful. He was a good and kind man and much loved by all who lived here. His name was Sund. He had a son, and the boy was very spoiled. As the only son of Sund, Fam got whatever his heart desired. And Fam's heart was not good like his father's. As time went on, Sund became old and passed on to the Other Land. Sadly, because Fam was the only child of Sund, he became the ruler of Jin. Where Sund was patient, kind, and loved by all, Fam was the opposite. It was a puzzle to many how such a good man could sire such bad offspring."

Quinn continued. "Fam was not content that life in Jin was simple and quiet. There was a general happiness in the land, and that annoyed him. He had often been heard to say that he wanted excitement in his life. When Fam took over his father's reign, the peace and quiet vanished. Fam stopped the frequent festivals that the people enjoyed and participated in and replaced them with war games. That upset the whole population as war in any form had been banished from Jin. Fam forced individuals from many areas of the country to compete in these games. The few that relished the idea of combat were usually the victors in their battles. Fam also introduced monsters of old to Jin. There was a time, years ago, when creatures of horror roamed the land. The good ruler of Jin, Sund, sent warriors out to kill the monsters, thus ensuring safety in the land."

Alex patiently waited for the rest of the story. Quinn took a long drink of water and smiled. He handed a cup to Alex. Alex took it gratefully and drank of it. He was enjoying the stories that Quinn shared with him and had to keep reminding himself that this was not a dream. He felt safe and happy when he was around this old man; he thought this must be what it would be like to have a father or grandfather, and he wished Quinn could go home and live with him.

Alex asked the king, "I saw a statue of a doe and buck deer in the temple, and they were not monsters. What were they for? They didn't seem to fit in as the other statues were hideous, except for a few that looked like angels."

Quinn looked at Alex and replied, "There was a story that was told long ago. The story goes that there was a beautiful princess from another kingdom far away from Jin. Fam had her captured as he wanted to make her his bride. She would not come on her own; she hated everything he stood for. When she refused to marry him, he had a bad man turn her into a doe statue. Fam figured that she would relent and marry him if he promised to turn her back into a princess, but she wouldn't, so he placed her in the temple. The buck was a young farmer from Jin that would not fight in the war games, and so Fam had him turned into a buck statue. Again, he tried the same tactics with the farmer that he did with the princess but to no avail, so he placed him in the temple too. It has been said that the farmer loved the princess and stayed near her to protect her. No one has been able to break the strong, bad bond of Fam, and so the two stay as statues. It has also been said that a heart of goodness and love would, one day, break the marble that encases the princess and the farmer."

Not enthralled with love stories, Alex looked at Quinn. "What other monsters are there in Jin? How will I get around them if I see them?"

Quinn continued, "There are serpents that are on land and in the sea, as you have seen. There are creatures that are half-man and half-bird. They are very bad as they can run and fly and are hard to escape from. There are flying monsters that are huge but agile. They often fly down and pick up their victims and then return to their nests to feed them to their young. There is a snake-like creature that lives underground that surfaces only at night. All these animals are carnivores and mainly live in the jungle. The fact that you saw the dragon near the temple is significant; most of their prey are taken by surprise. The dragon is one of the fiercest of all. He must have sensed your power and goodness, and it kept him at bay."

Alex was confused. "What do you mean, my power and goodness? I have no power; all I have is a penknife. How can I be good? If I had been good, then my room would have been clean, and I wouldn't be here."

Quinn replied, "I am not speaking of power as in strength or weapons. I mean power in the sense of being good or bad. You are a child and do childish things, which is normal. You are not a bad person. You have the capability to do great things in your life, and the monsters here know that. You will be a leader someday. The bad ones here want to strip you of that so you won't be a threat to them. They sense that you could send them back to the Black Land where they came from, and they don't want that. So they will make every effort to stop you. You have a white aura that surrounds you; I saw it immediately! That means you have the strength to do good for many."

Alex was speechless again. He could hardly comprehend that he could possess any of these qualities that would enable him to be someone great, especially at ten years old! Yet Quinn had told him that he was exactly that, and he couldn't dispute it. He would use the gifts that he had to get home and decided he would live his life much differently from then on. He would make his mother proud, no more prodding to keep his room clean or to do his chores. He would take care of his mother in any way he could.

"I have some items that may help you in your upcoming travels," Quinn continued. He walked to a closet and opened a drawer. From the drawer, he removed what appeared to be a stick. "I bet you think this is just a stick. But it isn't. This wand is special, and it will provide you with a barrier of safety if you wave it over your head. It may come in handy if one of those pesky monsters decides to bother you."

"Wow!" exclaimed Alex as he took the piece of wood from the king. It looked plain enough, and he could hardly believe that it could save him from the likes of the terrifying dragon at the temple.

Quinn moved to another drawer and rummaged through it. "Ah, here it is. I knew that this would come in handy someday," he said, lifting an object from the drawer that resembled a broach.

Alex had seen old women wear them at church. *What could an old lady's pin do?* he wondered, shaking his head.

Quinn turned to Alex and held the broach out to him. "This is a special pin, Alex. It may look like a pin an old woman might wear, but it isn't."

Alex smiled. Could Quinn have read his mind? "What do I do with it, sir?"

"I've had this pin for many years," said Quinn. "It was given to me by my great ancestor and was handed down to him from his. My great ancestor told me that it had great power and could be used in many ways. He had used it to cross the ocean of serpents safely and to traverse the jungle of the lion. He used to keep me up all night with stories of his adventures. As for me, I've never had to use it. The many atrocities of nature that we have had to contend with here have pretty much left us alone. Except for an errant bilbut, we lead a quiet existence. A bilbut is an animal that looks similar to elephants in your world. They are dangerous and have been known to charge many a lost traveler."

"Now for your question as to what you can do with it, I really can't answer that. My great ancestor used to tell me that knowledge would come to whoever possessed it. All I can tell you is that whatever it did, it did well as my great ancestor lived to be very old, which is amazing considering the danger he was often exposed to."

Quinn handed the broach to Alex. Alex examined it. He noticed that it resembled an old lady pin only in shape. Engraved in the pin's center was a picture of a warrior. The warrior was riding some type of animal, somewhat like a cross between a lion and a horse.

He thought it was the coolest pin he had ever seen. For a second, he could see himself atop the magnificent beast.

"Well, Alex, what do you think of it?"

Alex looked at Quinn. "It is the neatest pin I have ever seen! Do you know who this man is here?" he asked, pointing to the image on the broach.

"It is one of my distant ancestors, but I am not sure which one. My great ancestor once told me that the man on the pin was a great warrior and that he was of our lineage, but he never told me anymore about him. I believe I was too engrossed with my great ancestor's stories to ask more about the other man."

Alex handled the pin gently. He couldn't wait to get home and show it off to his buddies. He knew now, without a doubt, that he would get home. He thanked Quinn repeatedly. Quinn smiled and accepted Alex's grateful remarks. Alex then placed the pin on his shirt and double checked it for security. He didn't want to lose it; it was the neatest thing he had ever owned.

By now, Po had returned with a large platter filled with food and drink.

"Well, it's about time!" chuckled Quinn. "I know I'm hungry, and I'll wager you boys are too!"

Po and Alex nodded eagerly as they sat and dove into the delicious food without a word.

CHAPTER 8

W hen the meal was over, Quinn glanced at Alex and asked, "Do you have any more questions that you would like to ask me?" Alex was still curious, although now a bit tired after such a large meal. "When can I head out? I'm worried about my mom. She worries about me a lot."

"You can leave first thing in the morning, Alex. Po will come and awaken you, and you both will eat before you leave. I have steeds for you to ride as you will have a long, long way to go."

"I have never been on a horse before," grimaced Alex. "I don't know how to ride one."

"Don't worry about that, Alex," the king replied with a chuckle. "You'll be able to ride this one!" Quinn looked at Po, and they both laughed. "Now you have the rest of the day to look around the kingdom. But remember, the morning will come fast, and you will need to sleep and rest well as the journey that you are about to embark upon will be long and dangerous. You will need all of your energy."

Po interrupted, "We will be in bed early. We promise." He then looked at Alex. "Come on, Alex. I want to show you the castle."

Alex looked at King Quinn. "Thank you again, sir. I really appreciate all that you are doing for me. And thank you too, Po. I couldn't have asked for a better friend."

Po giggled. "Ok, buddy, let's go explore!"

Both boys left Quinn's stateroom and started running down the hall.

"Where do we go?" Alex managed between gasps.

"Follow me!" yelled Po.

The boys continued to race down the long hall until they were both out of breath. They stopped, leaning against the wall and slumping to the floor, laughing aloud.

After a few minutes of rest, the boys recouped. Po stood up. "Come on, Alex. I have something that I want to show you."

Alex stood and followed Po. The boys walked further down the hall and stopped at a door. Po opened the door and peered in. "Good, no one is here." Po continued, "Often, there are guards in this room for it leads underneath the castle. They watch for evil beings and creatures that try to get in from the outside. Sometimes they will not even let me in here! It looks like they are out for a meal, so we can get in. Come on, hurry!"

The boys ran through the door and closed it quietly behind them. The room was huge and consisted of a large table and scattered chairs. There were paintings on the walls of warriors on horseback, complete with swords and armor. "What is this room used for?" Alex asked. "And who are those people?"

Po answered, "The king has meetings in here. He calls it the family room. He says that the pictures are of his family from the past."

Alex looked around. "Where do we go now?"

"Over here," said Po. He walked to the corner of the room and pressed a nearly invisible button on the wall. A door slid open!

Alex's eyes widened. "Wow! That is awesome! Where does it go?"

Po put his finger to his lips to signal Alex to lower his voice. He waved his hand to indicate "follow me." Alex's heart was pounding. This was actually happening! For once in this crazy adventure, he was exploring safely with a friend. For a moment, he considered how great it might be to stay here and if there might be a way to return when he finally did get home. The hall was well-lit with candles burning everywhere. Alex wondered how the place hadn't already burned down. Obviously, the guards did more than just guard. They probably had a secondary job of making candles!

The boys continued down the hall. Giggling and making silly faces at each other, they never said a word. Alex felt that Po could be the brother that he had never had. He had never had so much fun, not even with his buddies. The hall changed direction and started to slope downward.

Alex and Po started down the incline just to have it level off and continue as a long, candle-lit hallway. Po stopped and pointed to a door that was at the end of the hall. Po looked at Alex and gave a thumbs up. The boys raced to the door and stopped.

Po whispered, "Wait til you see this!" and slowly opened the door.

Alex was not prepared for what lay before him. His face lit up with delight as he stared into a place that he immediately recognized. The "room" that he had expected to see was not a room at all. The door opened up to the field that he had daydreamed about while gazing at the doe statue in the temple. The grass was greener and plusher than any he had seen thus far, and the sky was a majestic display of pink and blue meshed together. It was as if he had returned to the daydream, and his joy could not be contained.

"This is the dream I had!" he squealed to Po. Po was all smiles. "How can this be?"

Po laughed. "I knew that you were special when you told me of your experiences in the temple. I knew then that you were meant to be here. Not many know of this place; it is very blessed. I come here a lot, always alone. This is the Land of Dreams, and it is the place that you were able to fly and see beauty that you had never seen before. There are creatures here too, but they are friendly. Often I come here just to be with the kunnels."

Alex cocked his head and frowned.

Po continued, "Kunnels are huge animals that resemble the dinosaurs of your world. They are kind and loving. And they talk! So, when I felt lonely, and I did a lot when I first came here, I would come and ride them, and we would talk while we walked. Would you like to see one?"

Alex was about to burst from his seams! "Oh yeah, I wanna see one! Do you think we could ride on one too?"

"I don't see why not," replied Po. The boys walked into the dreamland, and Alex was again astounded by the magnificent beauty that surrounded him. He had to smile at the paradox of the place—everything was real for a "dreamland." Large birds of unknown species flew gracefully in the sweet air, and he thought he could hear singing. It resembled the singing he had heard in the forest the day he came upon the castle.

"Po, do you hear the singing?" Po nodded. "I heard that same singing when I first came near the castle and also in my dream."

Po responded, "Yes, it is the singing of the forest fairies. They are beautiful little ones that fly around the forest and many other places in this world. Not all are able to hear them, though. If we are lucky, we will see some today. They are able to make themselves invisible so not everyone is fortunate enough to see them. The fact that you were able to hear them means you have favor with them. Perhaps they will help us to get you home. Anyway, come on. We need to walk over that ridge. The kunnels will be grazing in that meadow."

Po pointed ahead. Alex and Po walked and ran intermittently up the path that led to the ridge. They finally reached the crest of the hill when Po signaled to stop. "Look, there they are!" he shouted.

Alex turned and nearly lost his balance. He was speechless. There, standing in the meadow crunching on leaves from neighboring trees, stood three of the largest creatures that he had ever seen. The animals reminded him of the Brontosaurus dinosaurs that he had studied about at school. But these dinosaurs were even larger than the ones that he had seen in the books, and they were not the gray color that his schoolbooks had portrayed. These kunnels were green! The boys walked quietly toward them, and as they advanced, the gentle giants raised their heads in curiosity. They showed no fear or animosity. The boys walked closer still, and the huge animals started to purr!

"Don't worry, Alex," said Po. "That is their way of saying hello. They won't hurt you. They like people."

"Hi there, boy," Alex said while advancing toward the closest kunnel. "How ya doin? You don't have to be afraid of me; I won't hurt you." The giant creature lowered its huge head and looked straight into Alex's eyes. His eyes were large and soft, and Alex reached out and stroked its nose. The purring became louder. "Ha, sounds like a cat," he murmured. "A big cat!" he laughed. "Po, do you realize that I just told this big boy that I wouldn't hurt him, like I could even if I wanted to!"

Alex continued to stroke the kunnel's head and smile. "Po, just how do you get on one of these big guys? It's not as if there is a kunnel escalator! And how do you hang on when you get up there? Show me how you do it, please!"

Po answered, "Ok, this is how I do it. You pat him on the nose, just like you were doing. Then you climb up on his nose and onto his forehead and sit in that little hollow area on the top of his head. See? Like this." With that, Po climbed onto the nose of the kunnel and scurried to the dent at the top of its head. "See? It's easy."

Alex followed Po's example and within a minute was next to Po in the kunnel's crater. "Now what we do?" asked Alex.

51

"Well, what do you usually do when you want to go somewhere?" Po laughed. "You ask him to go and guide him by instruction!"

"You mean they can understand you?" asked Alex.

"Yes," answered a loud but gentle voice. "And we can talk to you, too." It was the kunnel!

"Wow," said Alex, eyes wide open.

"And where would you like to go?" asked the kunnel.

Po patted his head and replied, "How about if we just go for a walk? But not too fast!"

The kunnel nodded its massive head and started to slowly walk. The ground shook, and Alex feared that they might be jarred from their loft on the animal's head.

The view was impressive. Alex could see for miles, and the countryside was breathtaking. Orchards of trees bearing orange and blue fruits dotted the hills and valleys. Tall, thin plants resembling pampas grass swayed in the soft breeze. Alex was amazed by the color schemes all around him; the pampas-type plants displayed bright golden stalks instead of the usual wheat color he would have expected. Multicolored bushes dotted the landscape, thus rendering the countryside a virtual visual delight.

"Am I going too fast?" asked the kunnel.

"No, no, this is great!" responded Alex.

Po continued to point out the many objects of interest as they made their way. Small animals scurried away in haste with every step the kunnel made. They walked through another meadow and to a large lake. There they saw flying fish decorated with rainbow colors and snakes with legs. The environment was beyond description, unlike anything Alex had ever seen before.

"How did you find this place, Po?" asked Alex.

Po responded, "A long time ago, I was very lonely and scared. It was shortly after I had arrived here. I don't want you to feel bad, but I felt deserted when you threw me under your bed and didn't come and rescue me. You had put me under there before, but you had always retrieved me. I was upset when you never came to get me, and then I knew my time with you would be limited. I had heard stories from the other toys about the black hole but, like you, didn't really believe them. Then one day, I just ended up here. I have no recollection as to how I got here. I was scared as I had seen some of the monsters that you have seen, and I didn't know how to protect myself or what to do. Quinn rescued me from the temple, and I have been with him ever since. Anyway, I was roaming around the castle one day and came upon a door that led to all this, and so I explored. When I opened the final door that led to this land, I almost didn't go back. My friends, the kunnels, showed me around and explained to me that this is part of my world but a different dimension of it. They also told me that there is much evil in Jin and this dreamland was placed inside the castle to protect it from that. I couldn't understand how a land like this could fit inside a castle, but my friends here explained that it was all a part of the good here and left it at that. I have spent many happy hours in the land; there are caves to explore and many other friendly animals to talk to and play with, although my favorites are the kunnels." Po patted the beast's head affectionately.

Po continued, "There are no people here. I guess that is why Quinn places guards at the entrance to keep them out. Quinn knows that I come here; he knew it right away. He told me it was okay that I visit but that I would have to be selective as to who else accompanied me as the animals are quite fragile, even as huge as they are! You are special to me, and I thought you would like this surprise. Besides the caves, there are waterfalls in yellow and violet and streams that have talking fish! And flowers that sing! And groundhogs! They are white and silver and glitter...oh, you must see them! Kunnel, please take us to the place of the groundhogs!"

"As you wish," replied the dutiful kunnel.

CHAPTER 9

Alex sat high on the kunnel's head, his hand shielding his forehead as a captain would do while scouting out new waters.
The boys watched in silence, taking in the breathtaking beauty that
surrounded them. Alex was amazed by the singing flowers, the
sounds sweet yet energizing.

The kunnel tromped slowly on. The distance was indistinguishable; had it been miles or just yards? Alex didn't care. Every inch
of this new journey was delightful. Little animals, some multicolored, some plain, darted in and out amidst the gentle creature's
gait. Trees and bushes lined all aspects of the trail the kunnel took.
Ahead, a splendid hill emerged, and Alex was suddenly anxious as
to if the kunnel could indeed climb such a steep slope. Po instinc-
tively responded.

"Alex, don't worry! This guy can climb that hill with ease.
We'll be ok!"

Alex retorted, "Wow, was I that obvious? That's a pretty steep hill, alright. When he gets to the top, we'll be sitting pretty high too! Gotta admit—I'm kinda scared."

"Don't worry, friend. He will get us there safely. Just hang on!"

The kunnel kept up his slow, steady pace and crept up the ever-steep hillside while Alex closed his eyes and opted to peek now and then.

The kunnel came to a stop. Po prodded Alex. "Take a look at that," he said, his arm pointing straight ahead.

Alex stiffened and nearly toppled off the kunnel's crater. Now ahead, instead of a hillside, was a valley pasture of blue and green grass. Alex stared at it all. "What are those?" Alex asked, pointing ahead. "Those dots over there?"

Po laughed. "Those 'dots' are groundhogs! But these are unlike any groundhog you've ever seen! They have wings and can fly!"

"Holy cow, I do see them now! Oh, this is unreal. I never dreamed there could be flying groundhogs! Po, are these able to be ridden, too?"

"Yup, they sure are, Alex. When the kunnel gets closer, I'll ask a couple of them if they will take us for a spin!"

"Ask?" gasped Alex. "These groundhogs talk too?"

"Yup, they sure do. Here we go!"

The kunnel came to a halt in front of a small band of quietly grazing, slow-moving, winged groundhogs. They raised their heads in curious unison. "So good to see you, Po," said the larger groundhog, in a deep but tender voice. "I haven't seen you in a while." Tilting his head, he continued, "And you brought a friend today?"

Alex was brimming with excitement. Never in his wildest dreams had he ever considered the fact that there could be dinosaurs called kunnels that he could ride and now groundhogs that talked!

The groundhog advanced toward Alex. "My name is Bin, and it is so nice to meet you. Po and I have been friends for many years, and I know we will be friends, too."

Alex stammered while Po smiled. "My name is Alex, and I can't believe that I'm really talking to you! I've read about groundhogs in some of my books at school but never, ever believed that they could talk or fly! This is the coolest day of my life!"

Bin smiled. "I hope that you will like it here. We don't see many visitors except for Po. We have been in the valley for thousands of years; the valley is expansive, and we have room for all. There are many of us. We have a happy, peaceful existence as long as we stay here. We don't like to be near Nor." Bin shook his head. "Ha, I'm getting ahead of myself. Let me introduce you to one of my friends."

A smaller groundhog who had been grazing with Bin watched expectantly and stepped forward.

"This is Kea," said Bin as he nodded to a gold and pink winged beauty.

She spoke tenderly, "I am so happy to meet you, Alex."

Alex couldn't wipe the smile from his face. "Po had told me that you all could fly, but I didn't really believe that, and here I am, talking with you! And Po told me that you have let him ride you, and that is exciting too! Although I'm scared as I've never ridden anything but my bike and also the kunnels!"

The winged groundhog smiled. "Alex, we can help you to learn to ride upon us. It's actually easier than riding a kunnel!"

With that, the kunnel slowly dropped his head to the ground, and the boys jumped off his crater. "Thank you, friend," the boys said in unison. The kunnel purred and slowly waddled away.

The boys advanced toward the groundhogs. Not knowing what to expect, Alex stayed a hair behind Po. Po walked to Bin and patted him on the back. "Good friend," Po said as he stroked Bin's massive back. "See, Alex? This is how you do it," he explained as he again ran his hand through the groundhog's brilliant strands.

Alex stepped forward now as Kea stepped toward him. "It's ok, Alex. I won't harm you," Kea said as Alex hesitantly ran his hand over her back.

"Wow, your hair is so soft!" exclaimed Alex.

Kea giggled and responded, "Alex, it's not 'hair;' it's called my coat. But that's ok, you can call it what you want."

"Ok, now what do we do about teaching my friend here to learn to ride?" laughed Po. "I think it's time!"

Bin stepped forward. "Grab behind my neck, Alex. It won't hurt me," he said.

"Like this?" asked Po as he grabbed a handful of thick, hairy flesh.

"Wow, that tickles!" laughed Bin while Po smiled.

Po helped Alex straddle the wide creature and situated him onto his back.

"Ok, I'm on," said Alex. "Please, don't go fast! I'm a little scared."

"I won't let anything happen to you, Alex," replied Bin. Bin took a step, and Alex screeched. Bin nearly jumped. "It's ok, Alex. But please don't scream that that! You scared me!"

"I'm sorry," babbled Alex. "I'll try not to do it again. Ok, I think I'm ready now."

"Here we go!" said Bin. He took a few more steps, and Alex contained himself. "Feeling better now?" asked Bin.

"Yup, I think I'm getting the hang of it now," said Alex.

Bin walked a short distance, and Alex began to gain confidence. Po was clipping right along on Kea and belly laughing.

"You will be able to ride like Po in no time," said Bin. "It just takes some practice."

"I don't think I'll ever be as good as Po," replied Alex.

"You wait and see," said the groundhog. "I think someday you might even get so good that you might be able to fly!"

Alex smiled. He was proud that he could sit upon the ground-hog's back, but he couldn't entertain the notion of flying on one.

"Alex," said Bin. "Now I'm going to walk a little faster. Just sit up tall and relax, and you will do fine."

Alex did as he was asked, and the groundhog sped up. Alex's teeth chattered. He was laughing now and having the time of his life. He thought that it might be easier if there was a saddle on this awesome creature but, overall, he was doing very well.

Bin acknowledged Alex's glee. Little by little, Bin increased the speed of his gait until suddenly, the groundhog and the little boy were not on the ground anymore—they were airborne! Alex started to scream and then remembered Bin's earlier request. So, he hung on with a death grip around the groundhog's thick neck. He looked straight ahead, scared to death but still excited. He wasn't yet brave enough to look down.

Bin tried to soothe Alex's terror. "Just try to relax and enjoy the ride," said Bin. "I won't let you fall off. Po was the same way the first time he went up. After a while, you won't even notice the height."

Alex gulped. "I don't think I will ever get used to this!"

Kea flew up next to Bin, and Po attempted to get Alex's attention. "Isn't this a blast?" Po shouted. He immediately started to giggle, "Look, no hands!" Po waved both hands over his head, and Kea smiled. Alex started to relax but still had a death grip on the groundhog.

"I can't do that!" Alex shouted back to Po.

"You will, you wait and see," replied Po.

The boys started to laugh, and the groundhogs soared higher over trees and through clouds. Alex could see mountains in the distance. He was amazed by this as he remembered that he had gained access to all this beautiful land through a door in the castle.

CHAPTER 10

Alex looked at Po and pointed ahead of them. "Po, what's behind those huge mountains? Can we fly there?"

The smile vanished from Po's face. "Oh, friend, there are many places we can travel around here, but we should not go past the mountains. That is a different land. We call it Nor, and it is a place of bad. There are monsters there, and there is no happiness. So we need to stay away from there. And I know Bin and Kea will not fly there."

Alex was intrigued. "Po, have you ever been to Nor?" he asked.

Po nodded his head. "Alex, it was pretty scary. There were no friends there; they were all dressed in dark clothes, and there were no pretty plants or animals. The animals were monsters like nothing I've ever seen. They had many heads and tails and spit fire and goo. And they all flew and were very fast. I made the mistake of wanting to explore the mountain range, so I flew with Bin, even though he didn't want to take me. When we landed, we were attacked by demons, and I was terrified. Bin picked me up by my britches and threw me onto his back, and we flew away. I will never go back there again! It was so bad."

"Wow, that sounds really scary, but I can understand why you would want to explore it. I would want to check it out, too. Do you think that there are people who are trapped there? We don't have to go over the mountains for me to get home, do we?" asked Alex.

"Well, I've heard that there are some good folks who explored like I did and then were trapped there, but Quinn would not send soldiers to rescue them for fear of their safety. And no! We do not have to go into the mountains for you to get home, but we do have to go around them."

"Po, is there no way to help the people who might still be in there? That makes me sad, wondering if they are still alive or if the monsters got them already."

Po shook his head. "Well, if they are still in there and alive, I would be surprised. But if the king is afraid to send soldiers in there, then we sure can't take the chance."

By now, the groundhogs had done a flyby past the mountains and were over the pasture again. Po mentioned to Alex that it was getting time to land and head back to the main castle. The groundhogs landed at the request of the boys, and both boys dismounted.

"That was the coolest thing I have ever done in my life!" exclaimed Alex. "And thank you for teaching me how to ride," he nodded at Bin and Po. "I will never forget this as long as I live!"

Bin smiled, and Alex again patted his back.

Continuing to walk in the pasture, Alex had to pinch himself again that all this magnificence was contained inside a room in a castle! Soon the boys came to the entrance door, and two soldiers greeted them. Po introduced them to Alex, and they shook hands, and the soldiers tipped their hats.

Alex laughed as they entered the hallway. "I can only imagine what will pop up next!"

CHAPTER 11

Alex smiled at Po. "So, brother, what is the plan now?"

"Well, I think it's time to rest so we can get a head start on getting you home," replied Po. "But I think we need to have some dinner first! Sound good?"

Alex was famished. Po pulled out two small sacks packed with food. "Bet you didn't think I would bring us food, right?"

Alex laughed as he reached for the bag. "So glad you did! I'm starving!"

The boys ate silently. After finishing their drinks, they got up and headed down the hall. Po walked to two adjoining doors, opened them, and waved Alex to one of them. "The day has flown by, and it's time to rest as morning will be here soon," said Po. Alex entered the comfortable room, lay down on the soft bed, and immediately fell asleep.

Morning came, and Alex awoke to fresh food and clean clothing. As he nibbled his banana, a soft knock came to his door. Alex opened the door to find Po smiling.

"Are you finally up?" he joked. Alex laughed, banana and all! "It's time to go!" Po waved toward the hallway, and Alex followed him. "I've got us some food, and we have friends waiting, too," continued Po.

There in the hallway, waiting patiently, were Kea and Bin. The boys walked to the groundhogs. Po jumped onto Kea's back, and Alex followed suit with Bin.

CHAPTER 12

Bin and Kea walked the grassy trail that led away from the castle. Alex again grabbed Bin's sturdy flesh to steady himself. Turning to Po, he asked, "How do you know if this is the right trail for us to start on?"

"Well, I just have an idea it's the right one. We have no maps here, and the cave room you first entered to come here is pretty far away. Bin and Kea have explored more of my land than even I have; I guess that's because they can fly. I explained to them where we need to go and that we need to stay away from Nor. I trust them, and I know between the three of us, we will get you home. Let me remind you again though, while most of Jin is good, there is still evil that has escaped Nor and lingers here. And some of the bad disguises itself as good, too. Just follow me, Alex, and hang on tight!"

With that, Po dug a heel into Kea's side and urged her to a fast walk. Bin immediately followed suit amidst Alex's startled scream. "Whoa, whoa!" he hollered.

Bin laughed. "Hang on, Alex!"

The groundhogs kept up the pace for a short time and then slowed to rest. The trail continued and then came to a fork. Alex looked at Po. "Which way now?" he asked.

"Well, I believe we need to veer to the left," said Po. And with that, the groundhogs started down the grassy trail. Po continued, "Soon we will be entering deep woods. Parts of these woods have almost no light; the trees are so dense. And there are many trails, so I will have to be careful not to get confused. I think we will need to travel slower when we enter the forest; it will be safer that way."

Alex looked at Po. "If it's so dark, how will we be able to see? And what if there are monsters lurking in the dark?"

Po answered, "I'm not going to answer that, Alex, for soon you will see for yourself."

The boys rode in silence, Alex anxiously glancing to his right and left. After a short distance, he noticed a wood line of large, leafy trees.

Po broke the silence. "Ok, Alex, here we go. We will continue to follow this trail, but keep your eyes open. Our groundhog friends will most likely alert us to anything unusual, but we need to stand guard, too."

Alex reached into his pocket and felt for his penknife. Knowing it wouldn't be much protection against a 5,000-pound dragon, he still felt comfort knowing it was near.

The groundhogs walked on, the trail becoming darker and darker the further they ventured. Just as Alex was about to mention his discomfort with the sullen darkness, tiny flicks of moving light appeared before him, lighting up the entire path! Eyes wide open, Alex attempted to speak, but Po interrupted. "This is the surprise I wanted you to see, Alex!" he said excitedly.

"But what are they, and how can something so small make so much light?" Alex responded.

Po continued, "These are singing lites, or at least that is what I call them! They are tiny and flit around like bees, but they can light up miles of path! And they sing, too! So we get light and music at the same time!"

Alex strained to hear and broke into a huge smile as the delightful music became louder and louder. It was as if there were angels singing and orchestra backing them up! Bin and Kea muttered in tune with them, and soon, Alex and Po chimed in, too. The denser the woods became, the more light the singing lites emitted.

The group continued to sing for what seemed like miles, the trail easily seen and the woods breathtakingly beautiful. There were birds with multicolored wings that flew amongst them, and tiny creatures ran to and fro on their trail. Alex was amazed to note that without the brilliance of the singing lites, he and Po would be riding blind. The trail climbed hills and sloped valleys, with the boys enjoying every step of their ride.

Suddenly, a deafening roar erupted, causing their mounts to halt and circle on the trail, terrifying the boys. Hanging on to the groundhogs' thick necks with all they had, the boys gasped at what they saw. A globular entity emerged from behind some large trees, a huge shape with drooping eyes and numerous tentacles grabbing at anything within its reach while screeching noise from a formless, invisible mouth. The creature slithered toward the boys' mounts, causing further terror for the groundhogs and the riders.

"Follow me!" screamed Po.

"What is that thing?" shouted Alex.

"We gotta get outta here now!" hollered Po. "This is bad! I don't have time to explain. Follow me!"

Both groundhogs backed and bolted through some bushes to a trail that ran parallel to the one they had just been on. Alex glanced over his shoulder to see the glob gaining momentum behind them. The groundhogs suddenly became airborne, gaining altitude with every flap of their wings.

Soon the glob was a distant, screeching dot, and Alex felt that he could breathe again. The groundhogs continued their flight upward for a short time and then leveled off.

"I think we can start to land now. We are far enough away," Po announced. With a tap on their necks, the groundhogs descended and landed on a grassy knoll. They immediately started to graze.

The boys slid from their mounts, and Alex blurted, "What the heck was that thing? I thought we were in a safe place as we weren't in the mountains or past the mountains. I've never been so scared in my life!"

Po replied thoughtfully, "Alex, this is bad. There aren't supposed to be any jonos here. Remember what I told you about the good here but there could be bad, too? Well, you just saw the bad. But I'm shocked that it was here. I've never seen a jonos this far inland from the mountains!"

"What the heck is a jonos?" gasped Alex.

"Well, as you've seen, it isn't anything good. Jonos are monster globs that have been around for centuries, and they hate anything good. And that is what has me worried, Alex. You have a very good heart and are a good friend. And the only thing that makes sense here is that it was after you! Which means we are in trouble. I know that there are many of them in the mountains but, as I've said, I've never seen them around here before. And if there is one, then there will be more. We are gonna have to be on high alert and very careful. Boy, am I glad our buddies can fly. I'd hate to think what could have happened if they hadn't taken us up."

"Ok, Po, now I'm really scared! You're sayin these monster globs might be after me, and I have no idea what they do that is so bad! Just what do they do?"

Po looked at Alex and scrunched his mouth. "I've never witnessed this myself, but Quinn has told me about them. He told me to never go into the mountains because of them. He told me that they hunt the good souls and then grab them with their tentacles, and then the victim disappears. He couldn't tell me where they go, and I didn't push it. I never thought that I would see one, ever! So we need to stay clear of the mountains, which is a no-brainer, and be on mega alert on every trail. I don't want anything to happen to you."

Alex was speechless. It was bad enough to have that thing pop up out of the blue, but now nowhere was safe! This was going to be a long journey.

CHAPTER 13

Po and Alex continued to follow along the winding trail that meandered between lush woods and open valley, ever vigilant with every step. Alex felt tired. It was as if all the "excitement" had caught up with him, and he had hit a wall. Alex turned to Po and said, "Po, do you really think that I will get home? And how long it will take? I just feel so tired now."

Po replied, "I know you are pooped out. I am too. But I will get you home, I promise you that! And we have a ways to go yet. Unfortunately, we have to go around the mountains of Nor, and we may get a lot more tired before it's over. Just have faith and hang in there."

Alex nearly yelled. "Faith? What about faith? My mom tells me about God and stuff and how Jesus saved everyone, but I don't know if I believe in Him walking on water and all that stuff. And look at what a mess we are in now! Wouldn't God have bent down and helped me outta here by now? He took my dad, and it looks like I'm gonna follow in his footsteps soon. And then there's that

Voice! Is that God? Oh, I don't know what to believe!" And with that, Alex started to cry.

Po understood the frustration that Alex was feeling. He, at one time, had felt the same way, shortly after he had arrived in this land. Po answered, "Alex, I know you are upset; it's a lot to digest and understand. But I want to hear about the Voice that you just mentioned."

Alex dried his eyes and replied, "Po, there have been several times now that when I was scared or didn't understand—like now, but I hadn't met you yet—that I heard this loud but kind Voice, and he told me what you just said. He said he would be watching over me but couldn't help to get me home by himself but that he would intervene when he could. Ha, I still don't understand that. At first, I thought he must be God since he was invisible but I could still hear him. Now I have no clue."

Po stared at Alex and replied, "Wow, Alex, do you remember when I mentioned that the Voice might be the gentle doe statue that you saw in the temple? Well, it just came to me, but I was wrong. Let me ask you this, and think about it. Have you ever prayed when you were scared or worried about someone, maybe like your mom if she was sick? Have you ever prayed to God?"

Alex looked right into Po's eyes. "I'm so confused. My mom said that I should pray to God for guidance, but I never knew what that really meant, so I acted like I did so she would drop it. I did say a prayer once, though. I don't know if it was to anyone in heaven, but I did it when I missed my dad. And nothing happened from that."

Po replied, "Alex, regardless of where you've been with it all, God does know you and is here with both of us now! The Voice you have heard is Him. And by recognizing that and keeping Him in the front of your heart, everything we go through will not seem as bad as it may be. That is called faith."

Alex didn't know what to say. "So, Po, are you saying that it is the God that my mom talked about who is here in this crazy place?

But she says that He can do everything. So why can't He just take me home? Why does He tell me He can help with some but not everything?"

Po responded, "Alex, I really don't know for the God who is here can do everything! There must be a reason for the answer He's given you. Maybe He wants you to lean on Him, trust Him, and pray to Him, especially since we have to go around the mountains of Nor."

Alex didn't respond. He was irritated but still grateful for the guidance he had received from the Voice. "Well, I guess we'll find out in the near future," said Alex. "But for right now, I think we need to get a move on." Alex needed the distraction of anything to stop focusing on something that he had no idea about, and he was still rattled by the interruption of the jonos.

The boys no sooner turned another corner when three jonos flew in front of them. They both screamed, and the groundhogs bolted, dumping both boys on the ground. The terror was off the scale; now they had no ride, and these monsters were right in front of them! Alex was not ready to die, and he knew that Po wasn't prepared for that either. All three jonos raised up and struck out with their tentacles, their screams deafening. Just as Alex saw a tentacle come for him, he blurted out, "Please, God, save us!" And suddenly, the three monsters became airborne but in the opposite direction! Their tentacles seemed to get intertwined, and then they were gone!

Alex was in shock. Po was crying. Both boys were terrified by the sudden appearance of the monsters and then overcome with confusion yet grateful for the sudden disappearance of them. Po sputtered, "Alex, what happened? I knew we were goners, I have never seen the jonos do that—be in a group and so far away from Nor. I couldn't do anything; I was terrified."

Alex thought about how to respond to Po's questions. The only thing he had done, and really had never done in his life except for that one time when he missed his dad, was pray. But Alex didn't know if his screaming was really a prayer. "Po, I don't know. I remember hollering out, 'God, please save us!' And then they took off, all tangled up. But I don't know if my calling on God to help did all of this or if it's just luck."

"Wait, Alex, you called out to God? I was so terrified that I was speechless, so I know it wasn't me. It had to be Him. There's no other way we would have been saved like we were. Wow!"

Alex looked at Po. "Well, whatever happened, we are in a mess now as our groundhogs are gone. How are we gonna get anywhere without them? It will take us forever."

"Yup," replied Po, "we're in a fix now. And we are too far out for the kunnels to help us. Looks like we are gonna have to hoof it until I can think of something else."

"What? Holy cow, Po. We have nothing with us except my Swiss Army knife. A lot of good that will do against flying monsters." Alex felt like he was about to cry again.

"Wait, Alex, what about the stuff that King Quinn gave you?"

"Huh? Wow, Po, I had forgotten all about them." Alex tapped the broach underneath his shirt and pulled the wand from his backpack. "King Quinn said that he didn't know what this pin did; that knowledge would come to its carrier and the stick would provide a barrier of safety when waved over your head. All that seems pretty crazy to me, but I took these from the king so he wouldn't feel bad if I didn't."

"Well, Alex, what if the pin could bring us something to ride on if we asked? Since we don't know what it does, won't hurt to ask, right?"

"Hey, that's a great idea! Now, how do I ask? Do I do it like I did when I said my prayer? Oh, I'm still not used to any of this!"

Po replied, "Alex, I have no idea. Maybe you should ask the Voice and see what He says, if He will."

Alex looked around anxiously. "Ok, here we go! Please, God, will You make this pin give us something to ride on?" Immediately, there was thunder, and the sky that had been blue turned black. Alex looked at Po. He was scared. "Holy cow, Po, did I just tick someone off? The pin or maybe God?"

"Put the broach down and then ask me again." The Voice!

Po was speechless. Alex was terrified as he lay the broach down and blurted out, "Ok, God, now can we have something to ride on so we don't have to walk, please?"

There was silence for a few seconds. **"Alex, put the broach away. It will do you no good. I want you and Po to walk over to the cluster of trees at the bottom of this hill, and there will be steeds for you to ride."**

Alex was confused. He couldn't understand why the king would give him the broach if it was a dud. "God, why doesn't the broach work? And both of us thank you with all our hearts for helping us."

"Alex," said the Voice, **"I have always looked over you and Po. The king was mistaken as he took My blessings to be that from the broach. He did not know any better."**

"But, God," replied Alex, "couldn't You just tell him like You've told us?"

There was silence. "Ok," said Po, "guess we better get down to those trees. Wow, I'm just blown away about you talking with the Lord. I feel so much better knowing that He is really watching over us."

Alex thought about asking Po who the Lord was, but he kept quiet and decided to save it for another time; he had a feeling that the Lord was God but just wasn't sure what it all meant.

CHAPTER 14

The boys ran down the hill and into a cluster of green, leafy trees. The leaves were huge, and the aromas around them were like a combination of candy and oranges! As they walked further into the wooded area, they spotted, just ahead of them, a group of large owls. They both looked at each other. "Wow," said Po, "these are the hugest owls I have ever seen!"

The boys walked slowly toward them. The owls seemed to be pecking at the ground, but as soon as the boys entered their space, their heads turned toward them. The boys expected them to fly away, but instead, they just stood there.

As the boys neared, the largest owl spoke. "Hey there, young masters. We were informed that you needed a lift!" With that, he moved closer to the boys. Astounded, Alex and Po just nodded their heads.

Po replied, "Yes, sir, we do! We lost our rides when we were attacked by many jonos, and the good Lord told us to come here.

But I thought there would be horses here as He said we would find 'steeds'!"

The owl looked at both boys. "Yes, He told us what happened, and so here we are. Sorry, but there are no horses! Where do you want to go?"

"Well," said Alex, "I am trying to get back home and have no idea how to get there. Now I'm kinda hoping that God will help me get there. Did He tell you how to take me there?"

The owl studied Alex. "The Lord spoke with me and told me of your situation, and I believe we can get you home, but it will be precarious at times, and we have a long way to go. I see you have no bags for your food and clothing?"

Alex replied, "We lost everything when our rides spooked and dumped us—all our food, everything. By the way, what is your name?"

The owl replied, "I think we can help to replace what you lost. And my name is Ollie."

Alex tried to repress his smile. "How in the world did you get a name like Ollie? It seems everyone and everything in this land has a real different name!"

Ollie said, "Alex, I was a toy at one time. My owner was a little boy, and he named me Ollie the Owl. He kept me for many years, but eventually, I ended up under his bed and down the black hole and then here. And so, I kept my name! Ok, let's see about getting you restocked so we can get in the air!"

CHAPTER 15

Alex and Po looked at each other as if they were trying to ascertain how an owl was going to replace their clothing and provide them appropriate food. Ollie waddled toward them and motioned with his beak to a large tree behind him. The boys watched, amazed at the range of motion of his head! Ollie beat them to it. "And the good Lord gave us owls the blessing of turning our heads nearly all the way around so we can be aware of predators! And also of little boys who are lost!"

Ollie's comment broke the tension in the air, and the boys laughed while following the owl as he entered the tree at ground level.

"Wow, wow, wow!" the boys whispered in unison. They stopped and glanced around. The tree that they had just entered had become an amazing department store stocked with everything they would need to continue their journey—clothes, canned and packaged food, footwear, and even two pairs of binoculars!

"Where and how did you ever get this all together and even know our clothing sizes? And in a tree?" Alex could hardly keep the words from tumbling out in a jumbled mess.

"Whoa, young man, one question at a time! First, you have to remember that we are all here by the good graces of our God! And He was the one who alerted us that you were here and would need our help. He knows all. Where this tree was just a tree, in a second, He made it into a 'tree shopping center'! So look around and pick out what you want!"

The boys went from aisle to aisle, picking out pants, socks, shoes, shirts, coats, and plenty of food. There were even large backpacks that could easily carry all their goods. Their excitement was palpable.

"So, what do we do now? How do we get me home?" Alex asked.

Ollie tilted his head and responded, "Well, I think we better get one of my buddies to help as both of you sure won't fit on me!" And with that, he squawked at the rest of the other owls in the group. One head came up, and he waddled over to Ollie. Ollie said, "Ok, boys, this is Andy, and he is a good friend of mine. He has offered to help in any way you may need!" Ollie introduced the boys to Andy and then updated Andy on the boys' predicament.

"Ok, this is what we will do. First, you need to eat and then make sure you have all the necessities in your packs, and then, we are gonna leave here. We will fly around the mountains as we do not want to be anywhere near Nor. We should be safe that way. So go ahead and eat now, and then we'll be on our way."

Alex butted in, "But we were on the flying groundhogs, and this monster glob thing popped up out of nowhere and almost got us, and we weren't near Nor. We got dumped, and the thing was about to take us down when I yelled, 'Please, God, help us!' or something like that, and then they disappeared. And there wasn't just one; right after the first one, there were three that attacked us!"

Ollie pondered for a moment and then said, "Wow, Alex, you are being watched over! And we will need His help for sure; I have never heard of that many jonos attacking anyone, especially near here."

With that, the boys ate and then mounted the two owls while the owls gave instruction on how to do so.

CHAPTER 16

The boys found riding the owls much easier that what they had originally thought; their thick necks were strong and easy to grasp, and their backs large enough for the boys to sit on, even with their backpacks. They viewed the landscape below them for any anomalies, ever vigilant for any other monsters that might pop up.

After flying for about three hours, Ollie mentioned that they should land for a bit for all to rest and eat. Not seeing anything that could deter their landing, both owls landed in a grassy field.

Pulling out what was equivalent to an MRE, the boys chowed down. As Alex ate, he looked at Ollie and asked him, "Why do you think those monsters are in places they have never been before? Po said he has never heard of them being so close to town and away from Nor."

Ollie looked at him thoughtfully and replied, "Alex, I really don't have the answer to that. I've heard of the occasional jonos in our territory but nothing like what you have told me about. Perhaps there is good that is starting to flourish in Nor and they are being driven out."

"Well, as long as they stay away from us so I can get home, I'll be happy!" retorted Alex.

"Watch your backs! Danger is near!" The Voice! It was back! The owls and the boys turned immediately to see what was threatening them, but it was too late. Hundreds of jonos were coming at them from behind! They had no time to mount the owls or even run; terrified, both boys screamed and covered their heads with their arms. The owls tried to get into the air, but there wasn't enough time for them to get any foothold to fly.

Alex cried, buckets of tears flowing down his face, knowing that this was it; he would never see his mom again nor his friends at home or even his friends from this adventure; he lay his head in between his knees and just waited for what he knew would be the end.

CHAPTER 17

"**A**lex, Alex, wake up!" Alex shook his head and tried to get up and move away from the urgent voice he heard, knowing it had to be a jonos ready to eat him. The hands had a firm grip on his arms and continued to speak. "Alex, are you ok? Oh my goodness, Alex, wake up! Can you hear me?"

Alex now tried to push the hands off him. He opened his eyes and couldn't believe what he saw.

"Oh, thank the good Lord! Alex, are you ok? I've been worried sick!" cried his mother, now trying to cradle him, her tears dripping onto his face.

"Mom, Mom, what happened? Where am I? Am I finally home?" Alex felt his head, which hurt badly. "Mom, are the monsters gone? Where's Po?"

His mother, finally calming down, replied, "Alex, honey, there are no monsters! You fell out of your bedroom window and must have hit your head on something. I had come back to check on your progress with your bedroom, and you weren't here. Oh my heavens,

I am so thankful that your bedroom isn't upstairs! Anyway, I found you here in the dirt and unconscious. Honey, I don't know who Po is or anything about any monsters. Maybe you had a bad dream. I called 9-1-1, and they will be here any second."

Alex looked around. He was under his bedroom window and had dirt all over him. So confused about it all, he just sat there with his mom holding his head. Within minutes, EMS arrived.

The first paramedic evaluated his condition and said, "Well, young man, you sure must have had someone looking over you as this could have been a lot worse. There appears to be nothing broken, but because you were unconscious, we will need to take you to the hospital to make sure your noggin is ok. It's a good thing your bedroom isn't upstairs!"

The second paramedic helped to turn Alex on his side to evaluate his back. "Alex, what is this?" he asked. And with that, he held up a medium-sized bag. Alex looked at it curiously as he didn't recognize it.

"I have no idea what that is, sir," he replied.

The paramedic handed it to Alex. Alex opened it and gasped, his eyes staring into the bag. "I don't believe this!"

"What's wrong?" asked the paramedic.

Alex just shook his head as he knew the paramedic wouldn't understand. Every object in the bag consisted of a miniature version of all the toys that he had previously thrown under his bed. There were also tiny versions of the monsters that the boys had tried to escape from.

Alex started to cry. His mother asked him about the contents of the bag. Not knowing how to respond to her, he decided to tell her that he had found the toys from under his bed and was going to take them to his fort.

"What about this?" she asked, holding up a beautiful cross that she had picked up off the ground. Her eyebrows went up with curiosity, and Alex smiled. "I found that under my bed, too. Pretty neat, huh?"

CHAPTER 18

Alex was still smiling as he held the cross. There was no way he could tell his mom about how the great Lord had protected him during his perilous journey and how He had kept him safe from monsters she could never imagine. And with that, Alex again promised God that he would do whatever he could to help his mother—that he would never again lie or try to sneak out, that he would be the best ten-year-old boy ever.

The paramedics, after evaluating Alex, resolved that he was stable and should be followed up by his regular doctor.

Awhile later, Alex sat on his bed, still trying to piece together what had happened to him. And although he had no proof that he had actually been in a fantasy land, he knew that the objects in his bag were his proof that he had certainly been somewhere that was not of this world.

Alex then carefully placed all of the objects that were in the bag in a padded box and wrote on the box top, "Precious Cargo."

He then placed the box in his closet, vowing never to go under his bed again!

CPSIA information can be obtained
at www.ICGtesting.com
Printed in the USA
LVHW080021150620
658073LV00019B/1893

9 781631 292873